good deed rain

Q: "Ringo, why do you get the most fan mail?"

RINGO: "Do I?"

Q: "You do in Seattle."

RINGO: "Oh very nice. Thanks a lot, Seattle. I don't know, you know... Perhaps 'cuz more people write to me."

(laughter)

THE
BELATEDS

The BELATEDS © 2024
Allen Frost, Good Deed Rain
Bellingham, Washington
ISBN: 979-8-8693-4635-3

Writing & Drawings: Allen Frost
Cover Design: Robert Millis
Quote:
The Beatles, Seattle press conference: 8/21/1964
Apple: TFK!

The BELATEDS

Allen Frost

Good Deed Rain ◊ Bellingham, Washington ◊ 2024

1

Hilda

(1964)

1.

The morning had a miracle waiting for her. She came down the wooden stairs slowly, winding with them from her third-floor room. Winter made the house beams snap and creak. Even though she turned the furnace on, her breath made clouds. She clicked the kitchen light and the spartan room was lit by two one-hundred-watt bulbs. She noticed the frying pan left by the sink. The kitchen was freezing. Ice made paws across the kitchen window, also a frozen silhouette splotch of condensation that was shaped just like the photo on yesterday's frontpage. At least that's what Hilda thought of...four lads from Luddeshire... The Belateds. Everything was them lately. The newspapers, radio, television news and the talk at the grocery store: they were on everyone's mind. Not that Hilda followed rock'n'roll, but she could tell America was under a spell. She guessed there was good reason The Belateds were everywhere, with the president shot dead and another war on the way, they were the remedy for all that.

First, she went to the sink and poured water in the pan and settled it. The poet Mr. Mono left it there with soup in a ring around it. She asked him not to do that, but his head was in the clouds. On her way to the coffee pot, she stopped to look at The Belateds on the window. Up close it wasn't them, it was just frozen water. Still, as she got the coffee pot off the counter, she asked herself what she would do if it really was them looking inside. She supposed she'd do this very thing, make them some coffee. She reached up into the cupboard to get the coffee can. Wouldn't that be something if The Belateds were sitting around the table, chatting and waiting for their coffee? Or would they rather have tea? Probably. She opened the percolator and filled the basket with grounds. Then she poured water in a pan to boil. She didn't know much about The Belateds, but she liked their humorous interview on the radio yesterday. It seemed they wouldn't mind having coffee on the ground floor kitchen of a boarding house. She waited for the water to boil. The miraculous Belateds living on the window were beginning to melt.

2.

She went outside to get the newspaper tossed on the path. She was careful walking on those stones. Ice covered the neighborhood like frozen daylight. The dirt in the strip of garden was months from flowers. The cold leaves of the rhododendron were curved and praying. She bent like a windmill to get the *Herald* and turned just as slowly. Her house waited the way a parent will stand before a baby just starting to walk, leaning forward to draw her in.

Hilda didn't unroll the paper until she was back at the kitchen table. She still wore her boots and thick coat. The coffee was burbling and sighing warmly in the percolator. Mr. Mono didn't need an alarm clock, that delightful sound was his morning call, traveling upstairs, across the carpet and under his door. He would show up soon. Picturing him sitting there with his notebook and cup, she suddenly remembered they were out of milk— condensed milk, actually—that's what he liked in his coffee. From a little red and white Carnation tin can. She could walk two blocks to the corner store and get some, maybe before he poured. She took the rubber band off the *Herald* and flattened the front page. More news about The Belateds, the rest of the world was waiting on hold. WHERE'S HAROLD? read the black headlines.

The cold air still lingered by the door, circling her, and she put on her mittens and let it out with her again. Car tires crackled on 19th Street. A line of more cars were parked along the curb with ice on their windows hiding their seats and steering wheels. The bare oak tree hovered over the sidewalk like a skeleton.

She watched her feet, careful to avoid any arctic puddle. The sidewalk bore no trace of summer chalk pictures. No smiling daisies, hopscotch, or crooked horses. It was hard to believe it was the same concrete. Somewhere in the North Pole, the slabs were cut from an iceberg and laid in a line that stretched from her boarding house to the corner store. It was a long and treacherous journey for a can of milk. One day, perhaps a movie would be made, starring Shelley Winters, a pack of sled dogs, a background of painted mountains, and a thousand pounds of snow asbestos.

3.

The number of renters at Hilda's boardinghouse changed with the tide. At the moment there were four people living there. Herself, Gordon Mono, a college student, and an inventor named Jones. Also—it was hard to overlook—Jones had a roommate.

Hilda looked ahead to the next block and saw Jones tugging at a pair of silver feet. His roommate had toppled over onto someone's lawn. This wasn't the first time. The robot was unsteady at best, and it only ran for so long before falling down.

By the time she neared, not much had changed. Jones was puffing like a derailed train engine. "Are you alright?" she called.

"I was showing him how to shovel snow." Jones was trying to use the shovel to roll the robot over so he could get to the windup key.

"When is it going to snow?"

Jones rested. "That I don't know. I'm an inventor not a soothsayer. The radio calls for snow. I want Roscoe to be ready when it does. He could shovel the entire sidewalk. With enough winding, he could go all the way around the block."

"Can I help you?"

"Yeah, that'd be great. I just need a little more leverage."

Poor Roscoe was dead metal. Hilda steadied herself against the leaning shovel and put her weight into it.

Jones wheezed, "There we go! Hold it there!" and he kneeled on the ground and turned the key, once, twice, and two more times.

Roscoe shuddered. The red lights went on in his eyes.

They stepped back and made way for the robot standing up, struggling to his feet like a somnambulist just back from the other side.

4.

Hilda didn't stick around. There was no reason to. She told them goodbye for now. Jones handed the shovel back to Roscoe and gave the key a few more turns. The robot had five minutes or so to figure out what to do. By then, Jones would be on his own, Hilda would be having coffee with Gordon Mono in the kitchen.

And that's where she was. Hilda set the little milk can beside the percolator and Mono cheered.

She poured herself a cup and sat down with him. "Jones said it's going to snow soon."

"Since when does he have his ear to the wind?"

"I don't know. He has that robot, maybe it can compute the weather."

Mono took a quick sip of coffee. "The Earth is no mechanical thing, there's a mind behind everything that happens."

"Well, the paper is predicting snow too." Hilda pointed at the front page, "Look."

Like her, he noticed the same story. "Where's Harold?" he said.

She sat across from him. "Well? Where is he?"

Mono laughed. "Okay, let's find out."

As he read the story, a picture formed. While Hilda listened, a little movie played in her head. The Belateds running down the street, chased by their adoring fans, girls and boys and cameras. A Pandora's Box of energy had been released that couldn't be shut, that hollered after them as they flew. Music made an atmosphere. An electric cloud surrounded them wherever they went, city after city, country after country, freight trains and airplanes, buses and boats, until Harold finally escaped. Apparently. *The Herald* wasn't above speculating on something more sinister.

5.

The wooden table in the kitchen carried the marks and scars of cups and years. Gordon Mono had added his own scratches to it from paper and pen. He wrote poems on it at night, or in the morning when ideas were ripe. Someone could lay parchment paper over the tabletop, and use rubbing wax to pick up those words caught in the scrapes and whorls. There might even be evidence of what he and Hilda wrote to The Belateds.

One evening in June, the door was open to outside, blue and warm with the neighborhood sounds, the transistor radio was playing low and soft, and some relayed message caused Hilda to say, "Let's send them a letter!" Ideas like that come and go all the time, not everyone makes them real, but Mono was used to catching them, that's how he made his poetry. He looked for thoughts that jumped out of the ordinary and put on wings.

Jones and his robot came out of their room to listen. The laughter made Roscoe's eyes glow.

The letter was gaining momentum. Jones neared the table and asked to add a detail. Roscoe printed out the word "radish" and Gordon Mono worked that in. Hilda insisted they include a bag of Red Rose tea. She got tape from the drawer, "They love tea in England." Until finally, with moths hanging on the screen door and the sounds of night deepening to another level, they were done.

The unknown poet Gordon Mono held the letter to candlelight and read the orange paper. What rhythm, what rhyme, what a tip-tap, clip-clop meadow song. It might have seemed funny, these three roommates and a robot contacting a young rock'n'roll band, but they knew something was happening, they could feel it, and they wanted to be part. They invited The Belateds to come to the boarding house. How that could happen was just as absurd and fantastic as anything else and like conjuring any good magic spell all you needed were the right words, all you had to do was ask. The Belateds could play on the roof, there was room for them there, by the chimney and the TV aerial. Up in the airwaves, transmitting, with the whole town blanketing around, a haunted kingdom changed by a pebble dropped into a rain-soaked pond.

6.

When the *Herald* story was over, Harold was still missing, he could be anywhere out in the world, it was 25,000 miles around, and the newspaper was full of other stories to get lost in. But Hilda was still thinking about Harold. She was worried about him. She brought her empty cup to the sink. She washed it and left it in the rack. Gordon was busy writing something on back of an envelope. Before she left the kitchen, she stopped at the telephone. A tin coffee can sat beside it. Once a month, when she paid the bill, she emptied the coins. She dropped a dime into the can and dialed her granddaughter.

She was lucky Karin was still at home. She caught her just before Karin left to meet her local

Belateds Fan Club. They had divided the city into different sections, each club would search the streets for Harold. "I'll call you when we find him," Karin said. "If you don't hear it on the radio—oh, I have to go." Her mother was driving her to the park.

"Stay warm," Hilda said.

"I will," Karin promised.

"It's cold out there, I heard it's going to snow."

"I'm wearing my scarf. Bye-bye!"

Hilda hung up the phone. She had to smile. She was thinking of the long blue and white scarf she knit for Karin. The day they went through all the yarn at the fabric store until they found just the right shade. It had to look just like the one Harold wore on their new album cover. Hilda spent a week at the kitchen table, making a scarf long enough to wrap Karin three times. There was enough strung on her to make a fishing net. Imagine if by some chance Karin found him there by the fountain in the park and she caught him with that scarf. She would pull the wool in, hand over hand, until he came up close to her. Then what? A fantasy. Hilda surprised herself smiling again, thinking of Karin, thinking like a girl in love.

7.

The door opened and Jones came inside with a shovel.

"How's Roscoe doing with that?" Hilda asked.

"Oh dear," Jones said, "Am I still carrying this? I meant to bring it to the garage." He leaned it against the wall and rubbed his cold hands together. "Roscoe shows real promise. I expect the snow will tremble before him."

Hilda laughed.

"Now, let's see…" Jones remembered, "I came in here to get some oil. We may need it for our walk." Down by their boots and shoes was a cardboard box of cans.

She said, "Are you scouting more sidewalks?"

"No, no. We'll stick to this one. Meanwhile, we

have an appointment at the Avalon." He clutched a quart can. It had a picture of a red Pegasus.

Jones stuffed the oil can into his winter jacket. "If we start walking now, we should get there in time for the matinee." As he took hold of the shovel again, he sliced at the air. "*Sword in the Stone* is playing. It's a cartoon but I've heard it's delightful."

"You might see Karin and her Belateds club."

"Are they going to the cinema?"

"No. They're looking for Harold."

Jones didn't have to ask Harold-who? If you knew Karin, you knew The Belateds. Whenever she visited, the kitchen pans hooked to the wall echoed with their names. She left the house a reminder too—a postcard of them tacked close to the sink, held floating above the water like the jolly crew of a submarine.

8.

What does a widow like Hilda do with the day?
Well, it depends. This morning with snow on her
mind, she thought about soup. She left the house
and the house thought about her. The window on
the third floor watched her go, along the sidewalk,
around the corner and gone. That was the way
she went to the store. She would be back, with
groceries in a bag, it would just take a while. The
house missed her. A throaty sound left through
the chimney like a whale sighing far out at sea.

Gordon Mono was downstairs in the kitchen
with a cup of coffee, but he was writing and
somewhere in another world. Nobody else was
around. The housecat was already off on patrol.

The boarding house turned its attention to the backyard. Some robins bunched in the alder antennas. The garden was tangled brown for the winter. In the corner, there was a faint scar on the limb of the maple where there used to be a swing. Further in the branches a name was carved. One of the last leaves let go and fell. The grass was laying low. A snowman ghost from 1942 was waiting for the night. The house missed some of the things that happened before but there were new things to look forward to.

The house next door blinked, but Hilda's house didn't feel like talking. Do people even know all this is going on? The houses have lives and character—they are what you put into them—and when they're herded together in a neighborhood, they talk to each other.

A crow landed on the roof. It had a job. Another lookout crow was on the house across the street. Two other crows were looking around near the curb. They had to be watched over and if any danger appeared they would be warned.

The house thought about taking a nap, but it didn't want to miss Hilda returning. The window on the south side kept awake for her.

A squirrel ran across the street. A Chevrolet slowed down.

The house could drift back and forth in time remembering, but it was tied in place by telephone and electricity wires, cemented to the ground, it wasn't going anywhere.

A crow cawed and the four of them took off.

Hilda was turning the corner. She wasn't alone.

9.

A man followed her into the kitchen. She put a grocery bag on the table and he did too.

"You're not the Invisible Man, are you?" Hilda asked. She took off her coat and laid it over a chair.

He shrugged.

She couldn't help staring, he did look that way, face hidden with a scarf and collar turned up and that old fedora pushed down. Sunglasses too— who wears those in January?

He took off a mitten and waved.

"Okay, at least I can see your hands. But no voice, hmm?"

He dug into his black coat to get his notepad.

Hilda watched him write.

That's how she met him on her way home,

standing there holding directions like a tourist under an aqueduct shadow in Rome. He showed her the map. It was torn from a telephone book. The paper was folded and refolded and soft as tissue. A marker pen followed the street signs to where he wrote her address. More than his odd appearance, that's what really surprised her. She didn't have a room advertised, but he must have seen her address listed somewhere. Anyway, she took him home. No, it wasn't the sort of thing most people would do, but he came to her and it was cold enough to snow. The air tingled with that anticipation. He took one of her shopping bags to help out and she told him about when she was young, how she remembered there would be deer walking through here. That didn't seem possible now when cars were everywhere and the trees had been pushed behind fences.

He passed her the note and she read it aloud, "Hurts to talk." She nodded, "I know what that's like. Don't worry though, have a seat, go on. I'll make us some hot tea." Hilda went to the stove and got the kettle and brought it to the sink. Water poured from the faucet in a gush, a long splash from the reservoir.

10.

Marlin makes honey from the bees of the neighborhood. One or two always circle him in a halo or nuzzle on his hand. He's 92 years old. Sometimes he sits beside a table in front of his house at 3008 Edens Avenue, sometimes he leaves a brass ship's bell with a note taped to it: Ring for Service. When he hears that, in a minute the screen door will open and he will appear, shading his eyes. He takes his time. Time doesn't bother him.

Hilda keeps a golden jar in her cupboard.

His bees would gather in the yards and window boxes, ranging from the Good Shepherd Center gardens up to Roosevelt Reservoir, and all the way back to his house. Marlin kept a window open and the bees flew out and in, from morning until evening. At night they slept inside his house on the couch in a big ball like a Saint Bernard. And that's where they would stay, under a blanket, until winter was over.

But some of those bees kept him company. They flew around the house selecting from the flowers he grew. Lavender and clover filled the hallway and two rooms, wisteria hung from the ceiling. These uncommon winter bees made their honey in an old radio. It buzzed when they were at work. He had a teaspoon of that rare honey in December, another in March. It could possibly be the reason he lives so long. The magical power of bees. At the end of winter, another year older, Marlin opens the window and starts over again.

Just a spoon stirred in your tea would lift your spirits, would make you feel like an astronaut coming back from the moon.

The first snowflake was preparing to fall. It was a mile above town, looking down.

On 19th Street, Hilda made room for two cups beside the *Herald*, a teapot, with a glowing jar set in the steam.

11.

And he picked up a ukelele. It needed tuning, it had been lingering on the bookshelf for a long time. When he played it, the dust turned into "I'll See You in My Dreams." He wasn't singing yet, but when his voice was better, Hilda could tell he would be. By now she had a pocketful of notes from him. They crumpled and folded like origami.

For the first time in a long time the radio didn't need to play that evening. The TV in the parlor was a forgotten invention. The music created another world and they all got lost in the atmosphere.

Jones and Roscoe liked *The Outer Limits* at 7:30 but they didn't watch it tonight. They were living their own episode. A man and a robot, a landlord and a poet, hypnotized by music on a snowed-in night.

Their overdressed guest summoned song after song as if that's what he was born to do, like an overflowing jukebox. In fact, you could be lucky enough to hear it too. Jones pressed a Record button on Roscoe's control panel and captured the performance. He brought the reels to an engineer he knew and "The Kitchen Sessions" was released by DuCanne Recording Studio. The artist was listed as: ? There must be a copy somewhere, try the Goodwill or an antique store, maybe in a box at a garage sale.

And what about Gordon Mono? He must have been inspired. What did he write in his open notebook?

And what of the other roommate who was a college student who they seldom saw, who came and went like an astronaut cat? She wasn't there that night. That was fine, she was young with plenty of mystery ahead, and being out in the world held more allure than a kitchen in a boarding house.

And what about Hilda with her tea and honey and homemade soup and a pocket stuffed full of answers to questions? Origami.

12.

Hilda watches the snow fall past her window. 1964 was a long time ago. She felt that at the time: all her life she was aware of how things would come and go, moon rockets, Kennedys, wars, monorails, cats, people she knew, but she would remember the snow falling. The black window sky framed like outer space, the streetlights glowing on a thousand snowflakes headed for Earth.

Tomorrow would be new. The branches would be weighted down. She would get out of bed, look out the window and as far as she could see, 19th Street would be a snow-land.

At the end of last night, she gave the musician some blankets and the couch in the parlor.

She expected to see him gone, she just had a feeling. She got dressed and went downstairs and she knew the parlor would be empty. He wouldn't be in the kitchen either. The ukelele would be on the shelf where he found it. She would put on her winter coat and mittens and boots and open the door. In the morning snow, his footprints left the path and joined the white sidewalk that a robot would later sweep clean.

They would miss him, but they would also talk about him on and off all day and wonder if that was him over there, at the bus stop, or coming out of the five-and-dime, getting on a bus. It would seem like he never was. The sound of people laughing as they slid, a couple wearing skis, everyone acted like they were in a dream with dream powers. Throwing snowballs, chase, car wheels spinning, sleds jetting down where the sidewalk got steep.

So it went all day, until the sun was sinking and the world changed again. All the blue, violet and white, under the orange haze of streetlights the snowy night is quiet, quiet, quiet. A beautiful peace. It wouldn't last long, the snow in this town never did, the Pacific Northwest rain would be back and turn it all to slush and streams that would rush in the grates and sidewalk gulleys.

2

Mike Watson

(1992)

1.

The snow became water and the water ran to the sea and then it was time for spring rain. The summer came, the fall, and winter again. The seasons happened again and again.

Mike Watson saw The Belateds when he was fifteen. They played in Seattle at the Coliseum. He went with two girls from next door. They screamed on either side of him as the music shook. Going home in the back of the station wagon with the city sliding by the window, he could feel something happened. The magic electricity changed the city, like all the lights for the World's Fair two years before. He remembered walking under the gondolas suspended a hundred feet overhead, the roar of the roller coaster and all the noise of the arcades.

Everyone was happy. He followed that feeling as it circled the city and he rode I-5 down the coast to Oregon and San Francisco. He started a press and printed books. He went back north and the years chipped away. He had a job at a plant that published the county telephone books, junk mail, coupons and circulars. Then one day he gave his two-weeks' notice.

One morning he opened the door of his house and brought a cardboard box down to his Datsun. His wife and daughter weren't at home. He carried more things to the car, but he left all that space at the back empty. That's where the photocopier would go. He couldn't get that big contraption into the car alone, he was waiting for some friends from work. At least it wasn't raining.

It took four people to wrangle the printer onto a hand truck, wheel it carefully out of his house and down the steps. Lifting it into the car was hardest of all. They laid it flat on a quilt. Nobody was quite sure it could make the trip like that, but agreed it would be fine. An hour on I-5 to Olympia and another two on 101 to 109 to Pacific Shores.

Mike and his cat got in. Waiting for the traffic light, he turned the radio on.

2.

There were big wet gray fields surrounded by firs, black hills that soared up like Chinese paintings. Past Olympia, Mike pulled off the main road and took to a ridge of crumbled tar that was lined by trees. A stream ran on either side. A crooked row of telephone poles pulled wire deeper into the woods. A house would appear for a second, a muddy driveway, then more brush and shadows. He was getting closer though.

His cat, Lake City, was awake, circled on his coat, on the seat next to him.

Mike felt a long way from Seattle. This was almost back to the way it all used to be, not that long ago, tall trees tended by the weather. The road leaned to the left and Mike slowed down remembering that Steve's house was coming up.

No, it wasn't static on the radio, it was tuned to KAOS, matched with the burr of the engine. There was no sign of the sky except for above the road and even that was getting clawed by branches. A silver mailbox appeared.

He tapped the blinker and pushed the brake pedal. With a rented photocopier in the back, Mike didn't want to hit any puddles or bumps. The car ambled off the tar slow as a sheep. The house wasn't far off the road. Lights were coming from the windows, a curl of smoke left the chimney. Lake City was standing now, rocking on stiff legs.

Mike parked behind their car. He patted his cat and rolled down the window a couple inches. Without the constant growl of the engine, his ears felt the welcoming rush of the forest. "Stay there," he told Lake City as he stepped outside. His hair was brushed by the overhanging wet needles of a tree covered with diamond raindrops. A blue jay screeched away from him.

A girl appeared in the window and waved at Mike. He returned the wave. Steve's daughter, Gwen. She looked taller. Mike thought of his own daughter and it made him sad: what if she got older without him there? Steve dropped into view behind Gwen, a hand on her shoulder and the other waving, the two of them like a silent movie about flowers.

3.

Why Lake City? What kind of name is that for a cat? One of the guys at work found the kitten lost on the morning parking lot and carried it inside. Right away it went to Mike and Mike let it rest in his arms, orange and white and worn-out by the world. Mike's big flannel shirt warmed it up and it fell asleep instantly. Like a kangaroo, Mike carried the little cat tucked to him. He packed a box with one hand. He signed a clipboard. He went to the loading bay to look past the parking lot. A rush of ceaseless traffic. One was a car pulling in at midnight and leaving a cat. Then Mike started to itch. The poor kitten had fleas. Hurrying back inside, Mike held the kitten out and filled the bathroom sink and did the best he could with warm water and soap. The cat didn't mind, it let itself be cleaned, it was in a dream, and when Mike was done, he wrapped Lake City inside his shirt again. That became its name, from now on you're Lake City, Mike decided.

Lake City didn't mind the sounds of the warehouse. Moe Tucker was singing from the tape deck. A forklift chugged around on the floor. The hums, thumps, buzz and racket of work.

Nothing distracted Lake City. On a body of water east of Seattle, Lake City is the ceremonial name for a cement stretch of land along the northwest Lake Washington shoulder. Gas stations, restaurants, crumbling apartments, small businesses, fast food, auto repair, car lots, a Safeway, a bowling alley, a lumberyard, video stores, all the signs of the American empire. Lake City was everything you didn't notice because it was everywhere in America.   ·

It's a good thing Mike was there that morning. Lake City went with him. A companion in life.

After Mike gave notice, he put himself on another road.

Seattle was eighty miles away. They were in the woods.

Lake City watched Mike go to the house and get there just as the door was opening.

4.

It was good timing on Mike's part. A pizza was waiting for his arrival, Gwen opened the oven and Renata took it out. Gwen was also excited to cut pieces for everyone. She ran the sharp cutter through the crust while her parents chirped, "Careful," and "That's a good one."

Mike hadn't seen the family together for a year or so, but he stayed in touch with Steve. Steve wrote books and Mike published them. They ate and listened to Gwen talk about her dream. No wonder she's Steve's daughter, Mike thought, imagination was a cat that loved them both. Mike laughed. He was picturing Gwen in her dream. Her cartoon world was full of technicolor and animals and she could fly from thing to thing.

Renata got them cups of hot cider off the stove. The apples were from their trees, Gwen told Mike. He wished this was what it was like back in his Seattle house. Gwen wanted to show Mike her favorite book and she ran to another room. The kitchen was like a telephone wire after a singing bird took off. Her mother said, "Whew!" and they laughed.

"Actually," Steve said, "I have a book I'd like to show you too. Well, not a book yet."

But Gwen returned with the flock of birds that circled her air and everything she did. Mike laughed at the book she handed him. It was about weasels. He wasn't expecting that. "I read it five times," she told him. She wasn't much older than Mike's daughter and he missed her as he talked to this other girl.

Finally Steve got Mike steered to the garage. He opened the door and pulled a string and the room was lit by an overhead row of fluorescents. Gwen wanted to follow but Renata called her.

"Wait until you see what I found for you…" Steve shut the door. Another car was filling most of the floor. An old dusty red Beetle. Mike remembered when they were everywhere, but they were getting scarcer. A table ran along the length of the garage wall. There were stacks of boxes, three bicycles corralled between, a couple rakes. A section of the table by the window was its own little oasis, with a lamp, a chair and a typewriter. "Watch out for the skateboard," Steve said. When they safely reached the table, he put his hand on a paper stationary box. Ivory, 1 Ream, 500 sheets. It had the name of a store stamped on the lid, Fuji's Five and Dime.

5.

Steve worked at the library in Olympia, in the Underground Manuscript Collection. Mike always enjoyed hearing about it. Steve kept trying to get him to visit. There was a whole shelf committed to Mike's publications, and as much as Mike wanted to see the place, he never made it. Steve slipped the lid off the box and said, "Look what appeared at the library."

Suddenly something snapped like an electric charge, a jolt, the years disappeared, and they were back thirty years when Mike and Steve were teenagers. The box was on a chair. The chair was in a café. Gordon Mono was the poet's name. Mike remembered. He could see him. He heard his voice as he read from his poetry and put it back in the box when he was done, on the chair beside him.

There was always poetry before she appeared. Mike was in love the moment he saw her. A Girl and a Guitar is the name she went by. Mike could picture her. Whichever café or bookshop, park, church basement, concert or event she would be, posters on telephone poles, on the windows of stores, would lead him to her. He said hello. She said hi. He brought her a flower next time. She thanked him. He made her a book. She liked it. He made her a cedar box, lined in black silk, little tinfoil stars, with a croquet ball inside, painted like the world. He got up on stage after her and said his name was A Man and a Mandolin and he played love songs by The Belateds. It didn't matter. She was in love with someone else. He took a bus to San Francisco and never saw her again.

What happens to these memories that seemed so real? Is there somewhere they go, where they live out eternity?

Then Mike was back. Maybe only a few seconds had passed, but that's not what it felt like.

"You remember this?" Steve grinned. "We used to follow Gordon Mono around. All those places we used to see him with this box. He would take something out and it would be amazing." Steve watched Mike thumb some of the pages randomly. "I can't believe it showed up at the library. I tried to research him, but there isn't much, nothing up to date. He's in some little magazines and a couple broadsides. You should borrow it, read it, see if you'd like to publish it." He laughed at the look on Mike's face. "I know...I felt the same way...It's like seeing a ghost."

6.

"How do you plan on getting that out of your car?" said Steve. They were looking through the Datsun glass at the photocopier filling the window.

Mike was quiet. He realized he hadn't thought of that. There were so many things to think about and he just wanted to get out of Seattle. Getting the copy machine to Pacific Shores was miracle enough—once it was there what was he going to do, ask for help at the Shop 'n Kart? Steve knew that look. He laughed. "Don't worry. I know someone. I'll give him a call. He can be waiting at your house."

Lake City meowed. He was ready to go. A paw shimmied up the window gap.

Gwen ran from the house into the driveway. She was carrying a tinfoil triangle. "Don't forget your pizza, Mike!"

He turned and thanked her and that made her happy. It was raining a little. Wasn't it always? At least in the winter. The dark trees huddled in the gray. Mike said goodbye to this family that made him think of his own and wished he didn't feel the way he felt. He opened his door, careful not to let Lake City pour out. He put the book box under the flannel coat on the passenger seat and set the wrapped pizza on the dashboard ledge. It made a diamond reflection in the windshield.

It felt sad to say goodbye for the opposite reason that there was no sadness here. They smiled and waved and watched him turn the car around while the Evergreen College station played a record that sounded like a tornado zippered into a tin can. While it scratched and thrashed and tried to get out, Mike wheeled the car carefully around another puddle and checked the road both ways before he pulled onto the tar.

"Hey," Steve had said in the garage, as he put the lid back on the box, "Remember that girl you were so crazy about? What was her name?"

"Ohhh, I don't know," Mike told him. "That was a long time ago."

Clutching into third gear, the car passed a clearing with two deer painted in the middle.

7.

Along the steely Chehalis River, over the Wishkah River bridge, cormorants on the pilings, Mike followed State Street to the Safeway grocery. They were half an hour from Pacific Shores and he forgot to bring cat food. The look Lake City gave Mike reminded him of that. So in he went and out he came with a paper bag. Lake City knew what was inside and wouldn't let Mike start the car, not yet, not before Mike reached in the bag and took out a can. Lake City's tail turned into an exclamation mark. Mike put his finger in the pull-tab and pried the lid off. Lake City loved the smell, tail doing semaphore, but Mike had to roll the window all the way down.

While the cat ate, Mike had time to observe the parking lot of Safeway. Parking lots don't need a drive-in movie screen to tell stories.

To his left, gray going on forever across the car roofs and powerlines and low buildings. A factory was at work, one far out at sea, on a distant shoal where the ocean and the sky met seamlessly soldered together. The assembly lines flowed with rain and the smokestacks clouded out concrete colored sky to carry it. Ahead through the dots of rain on the windshield, a slow descending wave of rough dark trees met the town. Shopping carts rattled back and forth. A seagull on patrol walked nervously and stopped near a pickup truck.

A puddle lay in a dip. It probably stayed there all winter, getting bigger and smaller depending on the weather, and it took till June to finally dry it out. A girl in black rubber boots stomped through it. It didn't seem to mind. The waves calmed.

Kids were growing up in all this rain. Mike did it. They could do it too.

Car doors opened and slammed. Four teenagers laughed past on their way to Safeway.

Down on the floor mat, Lake City was almost done.

"We're almost there," Mike said. His mind went back down the road to Steve's and he remembered when they were in school in Seattle. The same sky. A Girl and a Guitar. Gordon Mono.

Mike reached under the coat on the seat and got the box. Fuji's Five and Dime, a store that was long gone. The box was fragile, it opened easily. He read the cursive writing inside the lid, "This is for everyone."

8.

A robot was standing in the driveway on Calawah Street.

Mike drove up to it and stopped the car. Of course this sort of thing happened in paperback books, but pulp was a different world than everyday reality. Mike opened the car door and got out. It was the end of the 20th century, you had to be prepared for signs and wonders. He said, "Hello. I'm Mike."

That was a good start.

The robot replied with a strand of tickertape.

Mike approached. The ocean air was marvelous to breathe. An almost ultrasonic breathing came from the sea. There was gravel underfoot but mostly it was moss. The robot didn't frighten him, it resembled a big tin can, one that had seen some dented years and rust, but he expected those arms were plenty strong. Why else would Steve send a robot here? Mike took the paper message and read it. "Good to meet you, Roscoe," Mike said. "Thanks for being here to help."

They went around the back of the car and Mike opened the hatch. The photocopier looked okay. It hadn't cracked like an egg and spilled ink and letters everywhere. "I have a good place for it in the house. I'll get the door open." The landlord gave him the key on a Quinault Casino keyring. Mike had been to Pacific Shores before when he found the house and signed the rental. He knew the spot for the printer, in the big empty living room, along the wall.

Roscoe clanked after him. He carried the big printer in front of him easily as a picnic basket. He was cautious getting through the doorway, turning sideways, gearing his arms and shoulders. Mike waited by the window. Roscoe's metal feet clomped across the blue shag carpet, leaving flattened prints.

"Right here, if you don't mind," Mike said. Yes, this would be perfect. In a little while he could go to Goodwill and get a table. A cardboard box in the car had the glue, thread and needles, clamps and a drill. He could start making books tonight.

Roscoe set the printer down and took a few backwards steps. He stood there like furniture. In the 21st century there would be no more war or pollution and friendly robots would be a common sight.

9.

"Oh no!"

The Datsun was parked with the driver's door open. Mike left it that way when he got out. He forgot about Lake City. The hatch was open too. There's no way the cat would stay inside the car. The new world of Pacific Shores was much too inviting.

"Lake City!" Mike called. The top of the juniper was hopping with chickadees. "I lost my cat," Mike told Roscoe. The chickadee song creaked like a carousel.

Roscoe swiveled his head like an owl, red eye scanning the low bushes along the house, the yard next door, the road behind them, across the street, and back.

Mike went around the house. "Lake City?" A tall cedar fence separated the neighbors. The backyard was boxed in by that same maroon fence. There was a tree with no leaves, no Cheshire smile up on a branch. A rope swing was suspended from it. No sign of a cat patting it. The porch was damp, no little Carl Sandburg footprints. Mike called Lake City again. The fence led to the front of the house. He checked inside the car again just in case. That would be funny if Lake City lay sleeping on the manuscript box covered by a plaid coat.

There was still stuff to take into the house, nothing a robot needed to carry though. Cardboard boxes, bags, a mandolin. Mike had to hope the cat would have the good sense to come home when it was done exploring.

He picked up a box and was going to say something to Roscoe. The robot was gone too. Was this a haunted driveway? Were they each vanishing one by one? He looked around himself. "Roscoe?" The rain was picking up. He felt it on his face and heard it drum the tin Datsun roof. He listened to the sandpapery hush of the surf carried on the breeze. The sea wasn't far from the house. The chickadees. Gulls. Then he took a few steps down the gravel and moss and he could see Roscoe going off down Calawah Street, meowing. It was a recording Roscoe had stored in a memory bank that was getting harder and harder to hear.

10.

Mike left the front door open while he emptied the car, and as he put things away in rooms, and got cords untangled and plugged in so he could test the photocopier. It worked. That was one less worry. He didn't shut the door when he went back out to the car. It was late afternoon and he wanted to go to Goodwill and the IGA. He put a sneaker against the doorjamb so Lake City could slip through. Where was that cat? It would be dark when he got back.

All the houses and low windswept trees were places a cat could be. And the smell of sea... Mike stopped himself in the driveway so he could breathe. Even on land, the ocean flowed and washed around the neighborhood. Lake City could

71

be anywhere, chasing the leaves that scuttled like crabs across the road, tufted by the breeze on top of a mailbox in the tide. The Pacific pulled at you. Mike couldn't wait to go walking on the beach that night. After all the manmade clamor of the city they left, this was like finding a dreamworld.

While he steered the twisting lane that led onto the avenue, Mike kept hoping Lake City would appear. On East Rain Street he had to slow down for a dog. If only he could roll down the window and ask if it had seen Lake City. There wasn't that much land before it became the sea. Would his cat go all the way to the shore? Suppose a submarine was unloading tin cans of tuna on the sand?

Mike found a good worktable at Our Madonna Thriftstore. Then it was just a couple streets to the IGA. He pushed a grocery cart along the white floor. The wax made a watery shine. He liked the oldness of the place. It was holding on to 1984 like a limpet. He tried every aisle. The front wheel jiggled and spun on its own like a broken clock.

He watched the girl ringing up everything. He moved towards her with the conveyor belt. He wondered what her story was. She had the greenest eyes. She wore a seashell barrette. There was something different about her. What was it? Something dreamy, something of this floating place. He didn't think she would survive in Seattle—a spell kept her in Pacific Shores.

11.

Mike thought about the girl as he drove. A part of him was still her age and wanted to go to the IGA every day she worked until they could say more than a sentence or two about the weather. But the years separated them and all they would ever talk about was the rain, the wind, the sun.

The headlights showed him the way. The twists and turns were new, but the road was one he had already gone a long way down. The white glow surprised trees and bushes standing in yards, but Calawah arrived and no cat. He parked in the driveway. The garage door was lit up by headlights. It seemed big as a drive-in movie screen just after the midnight movie reel runs out and the projector turns off.

He got out of the car and carried the groceries. The door was still open. Lake City might be home. What an afternoon Lake City must have had. The cat could roam in fields next to the Pacific and when the sun went down, he could find home at night. There were birds and mice, dogs, horses, loud tourists, motor scooters, and owls in the black tree canopy.

Whatever the forces were at work, instead of reading Gordon Mono's long-lost book of poems, Mike had a new project. He had to make a poster. The worktable fit nicely next to the copier. He spread out pages of *The Thrifty Penny* across the surface. From the cardboard box on the shag carpet floor, he got a brush and a jar of Mount Fuji Japanese calligraphy ink. Let's see, he thought as he held a blank page of paper. He was no different than a painter, he had to figure out what words to use as paint to fill the space.

Big letters, LOST CAT, at the top with a description of Lake City, Mike's address and telephone number. It looked like a circus poster. It needed a magician with Lake City hiding up a sleeve.

By coincidence, he set the paper onto the

table next to the advertisement in the Want Ads: "The Quinault Casino Presents The Beatles." A Belateds cover band. They were even trying to look like them. "Feel like you're back in time when The Beatles play. If you squint, you can *really believe* you're watching The Belateds." It was five dollars for The Belateds thirty years ago. Only a second to remember. He could reach back in time and still feel the light first going on.

12.

The poster turned out alright. Mike's first publication in Pacific Shores. Letting the ink dry before he printed more, he made some tomato soup in the kitchen, his first meal. The can reminded him of Roscoe. He wondered if the robot had any luck finding Lake City. With a red lantern light glowing dimly in front, the robot meowed and clanked among the streets, across yards and trails along the beach. If his daughter was here, Mike knew she'd be out there with Roscoe. She loved that cat. If he showed up in Seattle without Lake City, he'd never hear the end of it.

Fine, he thought, just let me finish my soup.

In the bleak quiet of the kitchen, his spoon scratched the bowl. His eyes went to a bank calendar from 1991 hanging next to the fridge. He could leaf through it and see what the previous renter wrote down and lived, visitors and appointments. 1992 was already two months in, tomorrow he could stop at the Bank of the Pacific and see if they had any new calendars left. He didn't expect to be here that long, but it was better than staring at last year.

When he was done with his soup, all he could hear was the faint buzz of the ceiling light. It only made him feel lonely. This is why people needed music and art on the walls and things to read besides an old calendar. He brought his dish to the sink and poured a little water in it. He sounded like Roscoe echoing across the linoleum to the other room.

The poster was dry. He put it under the lid of the copier and pressed 50 copies. He supposed his daughter would print the whole ream. If they were here, she and his wife would make a parade up and down every possible route until the sun came up over North Bay. He missed them. He imagined getting in the car, the county roads in rain, over bridges, finally returning to the house with his family.

While the pages were printing, flopping out into the tray like fish, another flapping disturbed the air. A thing that jittered with flapping turned out to be a bat. It barely missed Mike as it swooped past him into the folds of the window curtain. The unshut door must have lured it in. Maybe it was the smell of tomato soup. What bat could resist that? Mike pushed the door all the way open so it could see more of the night. The surf rush. A car churning on Calawah Street. "Come on, bat," he said. If he shook the curtain maybe it would take the hint.

13.

For the second time, Mike parked at the IGA. He reached over the car seat, grabbed a couple LOST CATs off the stack on the car seat and walked over to the store's covered entrance. He didn't see the checkout girl at the register. She had been replaced by someone who resembled a George Washington horseradish.

A bulletin board faced the entrance. The usual flyers were tacked: lost animals, job offers, cars for sale, music lessons. A bright announcement that The Beatles were playing at the casino. There was a space for Mike's poster next to The Pacific Shores Bird Watchers. While he was admiring the notice, someone else had the same idea.

A kid with a pompadour pinned his band flyer

at the end of the board.

Mike read it and said, "The Belaters?"

The boy nodded once.

"Like The Belateds?"

The boy grinned and admitted he liked them. We play a couple of their songs, he said. His band had a show in two nights. He handed Mike a flyer. Mike gave him the other Lake City sign.

"I'll look..." said the boy. "I bet someone will find him. Unless an eagle or an owl gets him." He paused. "Or a coyote."

"Okay," Mike said, "I get it. I know he's in danger, that's why I'm doing what I can."

"My friend lost her cat. We found footprints in the sand going into the water."

"Did she find her cat?" Mike said and quickly added, "No, don't tell me, I don't want to know."

The boy smiled. "Don't worry." He was dressed like a Cadillac, a look he took from The Belateds when they were his age. He could have been with them, shaking the ground with a new kind of music in a cavern under Germany in 1960.

"Good luck with The Belaters," Mike said. He thought he would rather see them than The Beatles. As he passed the newspaper machine gloomy headlines and went back to the Datsun, he thought everything's a cycle, we're back where we started, the country is in a dark mood again. He wondered when will something good take the wheel and steer us back on course.

14.

The Pacific Ocean started right in front of him. It was incredible to think it kept going on and on, next stop Japan. That would have been enough to think about, of the water getting deeper and darker with clouds of fish and whales submarining big as buses, but he was distracted.

Eyes down, Mike explored the ground where he parked, the path, the sand to the shore, looking for cat footsteps. Just imagine how hard they would be to find. Gulls left theirs. He avoided kelp. Sand dollars. Foam, flotsam, jetsam. The ruin of a castle with an empty moat.

He only just started spreading the word about his cat, there was still a good chance of finding him, but Mike had the sinking feeling that Lake City was gone, or if he came this far, he became part of something new. The Pacific. The sound of it breathed like a giant sleeping lion. Lake City was an ocean and lay purring and curling and growling against the land.

It was strange that Mike could see the beach so easily, there wasn't much moon on this cloudy night, then he looked up at the sea. The surf was glowing luminous green from phosphorous. Mike laughed. He had walked right up to a water borealis. Like seeing inside a laundromat when the washing machine windows are swirling with color.

No signs of Lake City. No cars, no cement. No sign of the Space Needle either. The wide sea would wash all Seattle away someday. He thought of what he was missing there—and what was missing here. The waves rolled in and receded, forever back and forth. The ocean never got lost, it knew where it was going. Did Mike?

With his feet sunk in the sand, he was watching an imaginary movie. The girl at the grocery, getting a bat out of his house, the photocopier, the phosphorus…and way back where time began, further than the stars of distant houses strung north and south along the sand, was a girl and a guitar.

Some rain stung his face. He thought about what it must be like when summer came and wondered if he would be here to see. The answer came from the sea. Out in the swells beyond the waves, the mermaids were singing, telling him, "Go home…go home…go home…go home…"

3

My Brush with The Belateds

(1965)

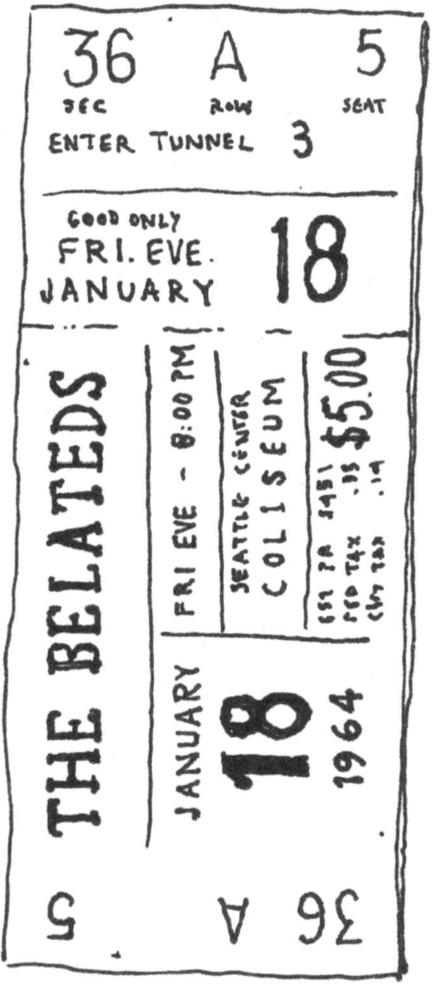

36 A 5
SEC ROW SEAT
ENTER TUNNEL 3
GOOD ONLY
FRI. EVE.
JANUARY 18
THE BELATEDS
FRI EVE - 8:00 PM
SEATTLE CENTER
COLISEUM
$5.00
JANUARY 18 1964
5 A 36

1.

There are times I'm sure when someone walking by on the sidewalk must look at our house in alarm. In fact, given the right equipment, Geiger counters and heat-detecting sensors, I'm sure our house must sometimes possess a signature not unlike that power substation two blocks away. A great orange flower. And the source of that frenzied, unstable atomic imprint is a girl of sixteen, our daughter.

Most of the time she's fine, when properly cared for, fed, pampered and allowed all the comforts we possess, but at any moment her mind, or her heart more probably, will plunge her and the whole house headlong into riot. Of course, there are all kinds of solutions to alleviate this, and God knows my wife has been standing in the height of those waves, trying to stay afloat with what now amounts to a library collection of books on the subject with titles like *Controlling Your Teen* and *I'm Not Crazy, I'm A Teenager.* But it seems like this storm is just part of the territory. Eventually, at some later point, we'll be standing in a sunny quiet landscape full of debris.

The cause of our daughter's outburst is unavoidable. It's something she sees every day, everywhere and everything reminds her of her obsession. There are correlations in any conversation, the whole world is but a reflection and no matter how small a fragment presents itself, it will set her off. It seems she is only put on this planet to worship and adore The Belateds. There's nothing in her life to distress and elate her like them.

I have to count myself somewhat to blame for this. I'm the one who brought home their LP, *Finally Meet The Belateds.* I couldn't help but notice many of the students in my class, especially the girls, overhearing their bedazzled conversations before the bell, the buttons that had sprung on their sweaters and coats like flowers. One girl had even turned in an essay comparing them to the Transcendentalists. Then too, I brought home a magazine from the grocery store with pictures of the band. That's all it took, our daughter was hooked. She took The Belateds bait and ran with it.

2.

At first it seemed like any quite normal fascination, and it even gave rise to what my wife's books would consider a bonding experience. We stayed up late the night The Belateds appeared on *The Sylvan Moore Show* for the start of their cross-country tour. I have to admit I pretty much ignored those four young musicians. I was watching our daughter instead. She was transfixed, moonglowed by their moving images on the television. Having them actually in our country, connected to the very earth we walk upon sent a current directly to her. And I'm sure it didn't help when I put up a map on the wall for her to follow their progress across America. She stuck little red pins in Chicago, Detroit, Cleveland...the tension was mounting...

they were closing in.

During that time, her fervor took aim. Four of them were too many for such a fierce devotion. She needed One and she found him in Carlo Abbey, the doe-eyed drummer. Like some sort of zealot, we watched as she papered her room with his image and her every other word of conversation seemed to include reference to him. He was enough to send her squealing into ecstasy and heights of fantasy unscalable by any ladder of reality. We put up with it...once burning, that fire was impossible to put out, it could only be contained. Barely.

When The Belateds were playing only a few hundred miles from us, I came home from work to find her seated on the front step watching the sky. A door opened in the clouds, with stars across the universe. In such a position of prayer, she could have been directly communing with them. Her heart might have been placed on one of those thick white clouds for the ride down the coast to where Carlo may have been staring out the window of his tall hotel and reaching out to her. Without disturbing her reverie, I drove up the driveway and parked beside her bedroom window.

Beyond the drawn curtains were her posters and photos on the wall. I had news for her.

3.

I came inside and announced, "The Belateds are playing here tomorrow!" What started out as a rumor became true. The students in my class knew about my daughter and her affliction and told me about the surprise show. That's when there must have been another power surge. My daughter tore into us. My wife was immediately on the phone, I couldn't even get my coat off, we were in high gear to find a ticket for her. When that didn't work—they were all sold out—we had to get back in the car and drive to the theater to see if there was anything, some last seat tucked behind a pillar or a row reserved for just such a sad case. The drive back home emptyhanded was nothing short of tragic.

Our daughter became a stranger to life. All her sobbing and tears had left her nothing but a shape in space. She went right to her room and shut the door for the night.

The whole house took on the shroud of an unspeakable grief. I woke in the morning, turned on the heat, made myself a breakfast of toast and left for work in the dark. It was hard to keep my students from bursting into song all day. Most of them had tickets and were watching the clock. But none of them could help me. I supposed I would have to try the theater again.

Getting home was parking beside a big teardrop in the rain. Her curtains were drawn but I could feel her presence in there, as dark and sorrowful as a cursed princess locked away. While somewhere in our very own town, The Belateds were having supper and tea, we went about the early evening chores in ghostly motion. We tried to coax our daughter into the living but it only started her crying again. It was her last screaming, dying fit of the night. "My heart has been cut into a million pieces!" She wailed her room and slammed the door. She let us know she would never go to school again. Hope had deserted her for all time.

I washed the dishes. I scraped the uneaten portions off her plate. I let the warm water pour over my hands and soaped everything clean and stacked them in the rack to dry. Usually I play music for this chore but not tonight. I was too afraid what memory the music might invoke.

4.

Finally, I got the car keys. I left my wife to hold our distraught ragdoll. I needed to try the theater again. You never know. Maybe a ticket would go unclaimed.

It was dark outside. In the morning I leave for work in the same darkness, with stars overhead, and here I was again, going out on another mission. I did turn on the radio though. As I reversed down the driveway, I recognized the song. It was a hit by The Belateds.

I don't know. I hoped our daughter would go with me on this quest. I wish she wouldn't give up quite so easily. She's got to learn to be strong. I know this world can dish out its share of unfairness, but there's also a miracle or two awaiting. You never really know what's going to happen. It's like the lyrics to one of those songs she listens to. Don't give up. Keep trying. The sun will shine. It will make her life better when she knows that's true.

The blocks around the theater were a circus. The Belateds had surrounded themselves with a magnetic atmosphere of joy and magic, starry-eyed teenagers skipping in packs on the sidewalks, the streetlights were blinking in all shades of color. I had to go five blocks away, out of that orbit before I could find a spot to park the car. Even so, I could hear the clamor as I stood on the sidewalk and fed some coins into the meter. The rumors were true alright; The Belateds had come to town.

I was in such a hurry that I forgot all about the rain. I should have grabbed an umbrella from the car. Anyway, nobody else seemed bothered by the weather, it only seemed to add to the scene. I was passed by more teenagers running in the direction of the theater. They fluttered and chirped like birds. A couple of my students saw me and sang out. I've never seen them that way in class. I guess they've always had it in them, it just takes something like The Belateds to bring it out.

I joined the crowd around the theater and noticed the doors were open, people were already going inside. The yellow marquee lights were flashing round and round. Again, I thought if only my daughter was here. Just to see this would have given her a thrill. I started towards a phonebooth, but it was filled up with laughing kids. I would have to wait, give this all a little time to settle down then I could try the ticket booth and see if there were any seats left unfilled.

5.

So I crossed the street. I stood under an awning and watched the parade. It really was hard to believe. The people going in those doors, onto that red carpet with gilded walls, seemed to be walking through the gates of heaven. When a pair of uniformed theater ushers closed the doors, I got back into the rain and crossed the street. There was a girl in the light of the ticket booth flickering like a candle.

I hurried up to her to ask about tickets, but she was shutting the curtains and I could read the sign she left by the window slot: Sold Out. Of course…Why wouldn't it be?

Standing there, so close, I could feel the cement rumble with the sound going on inside.

For the rest of the show, I lurked. The rain came and went. Sometimes I stood back under my awning. I went around the theater a few times, hoping that the big door in the alley might open. It wasn't impossible that The Belateds might come out for some air and some relief from the shrieking inside. They might see me standing there. Couldn't I wave and walk over and ask them for their autographs? Surely that would be enough to revive our daughter. I could finally go home and knock on her door and say, "Look what I found."

I was back under the awning when the ushers opened the theater doors again. I stood there and watched all those teenagers reemerge. Dancing and clapping and tugging at each other. It was as if a film had been rewound and now they were all coming out. It took a while, but gradually it got quiet again. They were all gone. But where were The Belateds?

I crossed the street. By now I knew those puddles like a map maker. I followed a rainwater stream into the alley.

6.

It was hard to believe this was the same girl as before the arrival of The Belateds. I used to read to her at night. A lot of talking animals and castles. That's one of the things I miss. If there was more I could do, I would. When you have children, you do whatever you can. You don't want life to hurt even though it can't be avoided. It happens to everyone growing, the birds and the trees they land upon. Learning to accept the good with the bad really is old as Mother Goose. Maybe this experience is what it takes for her to understand. I think of Romeo and Juliet, James Dean and Natalie Wood, teenage tragedies, when I see the joy and pain that Carlo Abbey is putting her through. She must know he's a unicorn, that meeting him is just about as impossible, but she put all her heart into him.

I know that heart, I've watched her all her life. That's why I went into the alley of the Avalon. I was Gilgamesh, I was Gawain, I'm doing all I can. The rain drummed from a broken gutter down onto the fire escape and I don't know what I was hoping for. Some miracle. What if The Belateds tumbled out the door and everything was put right. I wouldn't mind a fairytale ending. My heart was in it too. Just like my daughter, I was going to extremes for the Belateds.

7.

"Are you looking for them?"

I walked right past a girl without seeing her. She had a friend with her. They were both standing in the shadows under a fire escape. No wonder I missed them.

"The Belateds?" I asked.

"Do you think they might be coming out this way?"

I laughed. It was funny; I had become another teenage fan stalking their prey. At least we had each other for company, to while away the next half hour or so. Maybe it was longer. By the time all three of us were chattering with cold and rain, I suggested perhaps we ought to call it a night. It was late and we all had school the next day. Or rather today, for a new day had practically begun.

Out front, the theater had darkened completely. I walked past the poster displays, the shuttered ticket box, the chained doors. Either The Belateds were locked in, or they had flown out the rooftop vents. I stepped back into the street to take one last look at the Avalon, standing in the soft rain. Had they disappeared? On to the next pin on the map...

I walked looking for the car. In all the excitement it turned out I forgot where I parked it. The city was asleep. A mile away my daughter was too, dreaming I hoped of something calming and healing. All I wanted was her happiness.

Why else would I have spent the night in search of The Belateds and ended up in that café at 2 AM if it wasn't for her? I was hungry and cold from standing in the rain all evening and looking for a car that seemed to have grown legs and walked. There was a diner on the corner and I went in.

I sat down on the red seat of a booth and took off my wet overcoat. It felt so good to be sitting and warm. I ordered hot tea and rubbed a porthole in the window steam. The rain left hundreds of shining dots on the glass and the streetlights made little crystal balls of them.

8.

When my tea arrived, in a little white pot, I poured and cupped my hands around that ceramic mug like some shipwrecked sailor pulled from the sea.

The jukebox in the corner was quiet. I could hear the faint burble of a radio in the kitchen.

I did notice the bell as the door opened. I had been the only customer in the diner, but I pressed the hot cup in my hands and continued to stare abjectly at the climate outside. A rainy Valentine's Day. The Belateds had been and gone and what was left? Wasn't it one of their songs, wasn't love everywhere? All you had to do was warm up to it.

I didn't pay attention to the footsteps until they stopped. An odd-looking fellow stood beside my table. At this hour who else would you expect at an all-night diner? He looked like he fell out of a dream or off a carnival wagon. He wore his thick blond long hair like a wig, and a black, feathery moustache fluttered as he spoke.

"Hey, Mister. Are you nursing a broken heart?"

More than his accent even, it was his eyes that gave him away. For a second I felt like my daughter, with a bird's fluttering paper heart. Then I got it together and smiled. "Have a seat," I said.

And so he did and Carlo and I talked and laughed and shared cups of tea. I have to admit my daughter was right about him. It didn't take long for me to feel I'd met a lifelong friend. That's probably why it didn't feel strange at all to find us five minutes later in my car with the dawn coming on.

9.

We followed the headlights while Carlo dialed the radio and soon we were pulling into our driveway. I stopped the car halfway to its usual spot so the rumble wouldn't wake my wife and daughter. Carlo and I got out quietly as we could. He already knew what to do. We crept on the gravel, walking like cartoons, careful not to make any sound.

Carlo pointed at the window. I nodded yes. Behind that glass, only a foot away from her idol, my daughter was asleep. Did she have any idea what crept out here? Carlo reached in the deep pockets of his overcoat. He lined the windowsill with flowers. He seemed to have an endless supply. Then he put his finger on her window and wrote on the dew.

In letters that quickly turned to water, he wrote *Cheer up, Rosie* and finished below with *Love Carlo*.

He turned around to me, smiled and I patted him on the shoulder. It was getting late and almost time for school. That's where she had to go, and who knows where he was due. The Belateds were on a world tour. Next stop, Timbuktu?

I didn't want to keep Carlo from getting there. The raining had stopped, the morning light was pink and blue.

I would tell her soon. She could run outside, find the flowers, and if the words on her window were faded she could breathe on the glass to make them reveal. His message to her would show up again. Romantic, I know. I also know that this world has a way of squashing flowers and letters in dew. Failing that, I have a story to tell.

Then Carlo turned to me and said, "Is it okay for me to wake her up?"

4

Karin

(1969)

1.

Here's what happened to Karin when she went walking with a loaf of bread. Nobody asked her to do it and she wasn't compelled by wages or some strange responsibility. She was free. The bread had been cooling on the counter for about ten minutes, the sun was coming in the window and she decided to show it the world. She wrapped the bread into a shawl so it was swaddled like a baby with just a little window of wheat-brown face looking out.

Yesterday was cold and raining. She was awake all through that weather and was still awake as the dark clouds cleared and the sun came through the trees. Robins were singing for the first time, the invention of radio in the branches.

The milk truck was jingling up the street. All the bottles were bells.

It felt like the first winter day that shadows were back. A lot of weeks of gray when the sun is only a worn dime in the sky. She was floating along the sidewalk, taking breaths of morning air to swim her way in the 19th Street current. She didn't think about where she was going. Do fish? She would have to ask one. She glanced at the gutter—no minnows were in it. There aren't any street signs in the water, but she remembered that a salmon will find its way from a thousand miles away back to where it began. In winter, the salmon returned up rivers and streams around here. She looked at the next car passing by, thinking there might be a salmon driving it. A car filled with water? The windows were too busy reflecting the neighborhood for her to tell.

The little cowbells of the milk truck faded around the corner.

She pushed the shawl aside an inch and looked at her swaddled bread. Its eyes were open, a little smile underneath.

2.

The Good Shepherd Center is surrounded by a tall iron fence. The trees that hang over it are trying to crawl over onto Sunnyside Ave, escaping in slow motion. Karin pushed on the gate and entered the property, into a wave of sadness, the kind that fills jails and unhappy countries, like wading into a deep invisible lake. She knew the feeling and she knew she could walk through it. She held her bread tightly and followed a brick path along the edge of a playing field that was soupy from long winter rains. Some robins moved across it warily, looking for worms.

A couple crows flew over her. The blue air held them up.

This was a shortcut to another avenue where

the bus would be, and she was entering an orchard of leafless apple tree claws and her red crochet poncho made her look like the fairytale girl carrying a basket through the forest. A haunted kingdom.

The five-story brick building loomed through the branches, over the tops of tall hedges. For 63 years, The Good Shepherd Center kept the city's secrets. Sometimes Karin saw them outside, the so-called wayward girls who were kept inside— when it was spring they'd be in the gardens, when it was sunny you'd see them on the field, when the windows were open on the fourth floor you could hear their music in the chapel.

Karin remembered a story in grade school about a girl who got caught climbing the apple trees and was never seen again. That used to scare her, but Karin wasn't afraid anymore, she was old enough to know better. Daffodils reached from the turf holding flower buds that were nearly ready to bloom into yellow lanterns.

From the windows on the third floor where the classrooms were, the clack of typewriters chattered. Girls were learning jobs, laundry, sewing, housework, cooking, scrubbing floors and skills that could put them in office rooms, when there's so much more to be. Would their thousand typewriter words fly out like telegrams clipped to bees? Would Karin be able to pick up a page and read it, or would it be like something in a dream, that only melts away in this world.

3.

In 1969, the avenue was full of color. Time is a season. This was spring. She walked in a crayon box and stopped her shoes at La Boulangerie to stare at the window. Inside was a black and white movie by Jean-Luc Godard.

"Oh look!" she said, "Look at them all." She turned her bread so it could see the row in the bakery window.

I know from experience when you're taking a baby out for a walk, you're well aware that you're showing off the world. You want your child to hear songs and see pigeons and telephone lines, electricity, people who look like cartoons and be surprised when the troop of Hari Krishnas come chanting. You know these are things being seen for the very first time. At least in this life.

And don't forget smell! The bakery floated in the air like a lotus.

Karin pulled the cloth so her bread could see. She wondered if her bread needed a name. It shouldn't be an it! Funny, she had gone all this way with it and still didn't know its name.

When she went to Fuji's for Blackjack gum, the cashier asked her and she laughed.

How do you put a name on something?

There was every kind of bread in the window. This was like a look at heaven.

People were finally getting it together, they appreciated each other, they knew about ecology. Love is everywhere. That's what The Belateds say.

"Pumpernickel," she touched the glass and she smiled as soon as she did.

1969 was only a year after Martin Luther King was shot and when Robert Kennedy bled to death on the floor of a hotel kitchen. War was going out of control.

It isn't easy to believe in something wonderful. You have to open your heart and really, really, really and truly live in hope and make it real.

4.

She handed the driver some coins and the bus was ready to take her downtown. She found a seat and looked out the window. Something was happening. It felt like the bus was sitting still and everything outside was walking around her. The shops had feet like millipedes and were scuttling along. People bent in and out like birds. The sidewalk kept unrolling like a conveyor belt. Karin's bread was sleeping on the lap of her skirt. Everything revolved around her. She imagined a world where that was true, where the bus was a sun and the city went around and around. The bus made stops at Mars and Jupiter and Saturn and moons in between.

Who would have expected the #5 bus to reveal the universe?

At a stop on Harrison Street, another girl got on, with a baguette sticking out of a knitted bag. Karin watched her float down the aisle past her to find a seat further back. They shared a smile and the unspoken awareness of someone else who knew what it was like to carry a loaf of bread and care for it with love.

While the buildings danced, she caught a glimpse of the blue sea, the islands, a green and white ferry. She was almost there. Soldiers in brown uniforms bunched the corner on Pike. They would finally sleep on their way to Asia. Somewhere over the Pacific clouded their last dreams of this America. Years from now, when the winds are right and the rain is falling on your roof at night, you might find yourself dreaming one of them.

She might have gone a little far, she got off the bus at Pier 54. That was okay, it was a sunny day and the smell of the salt water was bristling. She crossed the street to get to the sidewalk that ran along the drop-off. She loved looking down at the emerald water around the pilings, the little fish that drifted, the purple starfish and anemones. Sometimes there was a jellyfish, sometimes a plastic bag.

5.

She wanted to take her bread to the waterfront hotel on Pier 67 where The Belateds stayed. That was a tourist thing to do, but it was fun to see other people there too. They came from all over the world to stand on the boardwalk with their cameras and point at the south side of the building, up to room 272. Only five years ago The Belateds were fishing from their window. Karin was here with the crowds that day. Oh, if only she could have been a fish, she would have gladly let herself go up into their air.

Pier 56 had Trident Imports where it smelled like candles, where she liked to spin very slowly in the round wicker chair suspended like an egg from the ceiling. She was thinking about going in the totem pole entrance of Ye Olde Curiosity Shop, she had been there before, to see the strange creatures in jars, the mummy, the bones and things that used to scare her. She wondered what the bread would think. Its eyes would be wide as raisins.

A seagull veered around her, a white flash as it went after something in the water. Another loud scream and her thoughts were torn to confetti by five more gulls. She held her bread with both arms and scooted against the lamppost.

An old man stood twenty feet away on the pier. He was dressed in a navy-blue captain's cap and a baggy suit and he was tossing scraps over the rail. He held a soup bowl full of bread.

Karin knew who it was, she had seen him on TV commercials. He was the sort of character a city should make a statue of so he won't be forgotten.

She was frozen, staring at Ivar feeding the gulls.

The swarming birds were going crazy, diving and splashing and screeching. He watched them with a thin smile. When he was done, he leaned over the rail and shook down the crumbs. Then he tucked the bowl under his arm and turned and saw the girl.

He saw Karin and he must have had seagull eyes because he noticed the bread loaf too. That's what he wanted. He pointed at it and shook the empty bowl.

6.

He had to be joking, right? Another spot for TV. But this didn't seem to be. The old man in the suit even took a few steps towards her before she was able to move. Bright and beautiful as it is, this isn't always a safe world, there are perils you have to acknowledge and adapt to. She tucked her arms under her poncho and fled.

Did her bread recognize what was being eaten in the water? Would the bread know it could have been next? More soldiers were coming from Western Avenue in their march towards Vietnam.

Escape was primeval, so much still is. That's how she found herself a few blocks away with somewhere to hide. Somewhere dark.

The Seattle Wax Museum is gone now, I'm not sure where it disappeared. Apartments have been built over its site and those stacked rooms are probably being haunted by wax visions of Abe Lincoln, Kennedys, astronauts, Jackie Robinson, Marilyn Monroe, and a cast of other characters I've since forgotten. I do remember The Belateds were there. In 1969, they had just arrived, they had their own room.

First she had to walk through imaginary rain.

A cold black room with a curtain of real water raining. She held her hand over the velvet rope and felt it. The museum even fanned in the smell of a bleak, dim, wet winter dawn. The first white settlers of Seattle have just landed on the beach, looking hopeless. A woman holds a baby covered in a soaked blanket. They're still in the rowboat, they're not ready to step out into thick mudflat. Their leader holds his bleeding arm where he slipped getting out with his axe, slogging his way onto the shore, where Chief Seattle is standing. He came out of the woods when he saw their sailing ship round the point and drop anchor. The smoke from the longhouse paints its way through the firs. The rain hushed. Karin heard a wax seagull.

The Belateds waited for her around the next dark corner. A record plays. Light is wagging like a cat's tail.

7.

Caught in a full bloom of blue and yellow light, The Belateds were leaning from a window frame. It was that famous scene of them fishing, a photograph made real, strange magic transforming flesh into wax. A section of hotel wall stretched from the floor up to the ceiling shadows. A fake seagull watched them from a nearby ledge.

She wasn't alone with them, ten or so other people gathered close to the red velvet rope, silhouette shapes against the glow. This was a popular shrine, she had made the pilgrimage from the real place to this recreation.

One of their songs was playing from hidden speakers. She watched them close to see if their lips were moving. The Belateds were four of the rarest birds captured in a foreign land, caged and brought to our shores, locked in this zoo, caught in the shine and amplifying.

A raucous school fieldtrip arrived from the other solemn room. The fourth graders bunched and bumped and spread along the rope. They were chattering, joking, laughing and singing along and loud as starlings on a telephone wire. The teacher, a young woman not much older than Karin, hovered about them. She was a fan too, she was wearing Belated Boots. For a moment she swung her long hair to the song.

It was an effort to get her flock to move to the next room. They waved and chanted goodbye, goodbye, bye! The Belateds watched them ever so slyly and couldn't help but smile. Karin smiled too. That could really be them, couldn't it? There was a rumor they wanted to see the display. Were they in disguise? Playing themselves? The rumors promised they would return. It would be just like them to replace their lookalikes.

They held themselves still. Their fishing lines let down like Rapunzel. Bright reflections from the imaginary waves danced on the hotel wall.

She still loved The Belateds, she always will, and she liked to think they would always be here, tied by fishing lines to the water and mountains and cedar trees. In another month she will be living on a houseboat on Lake Union, but she doesn't know that yet. Near where the Aurora Bridge makes a rainbow over the ship canal.

8.

Karin yawned. She realized she still hadn't slept and the bread was getting heavier while the street was getting steeper, nearly vertical. She leaned on the door of the Western Coffee House and went in. She was glad she did. First of all, everything had turned black and white. A cowboy hat was perched on a hatrack above a tasseled coat. While The Belateds may be kings on the radio waves, the air in here was an autoharp and Anita Carter.

A chrome edged counter ran to the back of the room, but Karin sat at a booth. What a relief! She put the bread on the vinyl seating next to her. Her back rested comfortably against leather. Framed pictures of roundups, rodeos, horses, prairies, lobby cards, old movie memorabilia. Studying them, she was surprised to see the murky photo of a gorilla holding a guitar.

"Hello, dear. Can I get you something?"

"Oh," Karin startled and turned, "Just a coffee, please. I'm so tired."

The waitress noticed the bundle. It took a lot to surprise Mary Quart. The swaddled bread was the work of someone gentle, she knew that, and she played along. "Is it nap time?"

"Yes, but not for me." She yawned again, she couldn't help it, "I have to get home first."

"I think I can help you with that," Mary said. "When you finish your coffee, let me know."

In no time at all, a thick mug appeared on the formica. The coffee worked its charms quickly and warmly and gave Karin new life, strength and purpose. For a second, she thought she'd like a piece of toast with it, toast with butter and blueberry jam…then she remembered who was sleeping beside her.

Horses ran across the wallpaper like a merry-go-round, rising and falling.

The bread stirred. Karin felt they better get going. She waved at Mary. The waitress walked with a campfire halo. A pair of quarters in 1969 was plenty for a strong cup of coffee and a horse to ride home on.

9.

Mary Quart held the reins toward her. "This is Melody," she said.

"A horse." Karin sounded like someone reading the word in a dictionary. "Right here in the city."

Melody was from Melody Ranch where a radio tower broadcast the dreams of an underground empire. Once in a while the horse took an elevator to visit the coffeehouse. There was a painting of her in a place of honor, by the kitchen doorway. She dug a hoof at the cobblestone.

"Ready?" Mary said.

Up she went and all of a sudden Karin was a floating cloud. She held a hand on the reins. She never rode a horse before but when she was little, she rode a camel at the zoo. Melody started forward and Karin reined her to a stop. "How will she get back to you?"

Mary said, "Don't worry, she'll find her way. Here—Take this with you." She handed Karin an old leather Pony Express mailbag. Karin drew it over her shoulder. "It's full of flowers. Scatter them as you go and Melody will follow the trail back to me."

"Like Hansel and Gretel," said Karin. She didn't mind being in a storybook fable, cradling her bread with one arm and holding on to a horse. A car went past them, bumping over the stones, missing them. Melody wasn't worried, she didn't have any trouble navigating Western Avenue. She went around pallets and garbage cans. Karin rode beneath the monorail up on an aqueduct, and under the gondolas where the World's Fair used to be. Now it was the Fun Forest carnival. The horse sailed across a parking lot, right by the man sitting in the pay booth. He was reading the *Times*. There were lots of people that didn't notice Karin and Melody.

Like Pegasus they flew over I-5. Cars roared and drew crayon lines below the bridge. Circus patterns, the colors of flowers.

Melody clopped onwards. A girl waved from an apartment window. A dog barked from the balcony. Melody would go from the curb to the sidewalk like an artfully sewn hem. She stopped a few times to crop the grass wherever a vacant lot grew and all the while Karin reached into a bag that never ran out of petals.

10.

A big laurel tree drooped above the sidewalk and the horse stopped to try the grass tufting from the cement. From her height on the horse, Karin could look directly into the leaves. The branch that stretched over the sidewalk told a story. You had to be up here to know it. Some kid parked a movie in the tree when they went home as it was getting dark.

Green plastic soldiers and dinosaurs were wedged along the branch and tucked into the twigs. Karin could have reached out and put them in different places. Whoever gave life to them and left them would believe they moved on their own. That wouldn't be a surprise. Not if you spent your days climbing trees and making believe.

In a neighborhood like this, you knew when you were in their world. Chalk drawings on the sidewalk, bikes left on grass, games overheard coming over fences, the appearance of a girl wearing a crown, a boy in a cape. Their imaginations were going all the time before the 21st Century arrived and led them all merrily into a computer world.

Karin wasn't too far from 19th Street and she told Melody this was a good place to stop. She looped the mailbag on the saddle horn and set her bread in there with the petals while she eased her leg over and down. What an adventure—a city where you could still ride a horse and see The Belateds all in a day. Her bread was asleep again, with some flowers stuck to its shawl.

Even if you know the city you've grown up in, it's fun to see it in a different way, pretend you're new here, let yourself think you're a tourist from Saturn or Rishikesh. Or like Karin, you can carry a loaf of bread you made and believe it's a holy saint.

A door opened across the yard and she heard kids. Maybe they were coming back to their tree and their movie. She bet they would like to see Melody, but when she turned around the horse was gone. Just like Mary Quart promised, Melody knew the way. Flowers were on the street, the wind hadn't blown them all away.

11.

Buds were swelling on the maples, and pink and white flowers were snapping on the cherry trees. In a couple months a green canopy would be pulled over 19th Street. Karin hoped Melody would come back. There would be a lot for a horse to eat by June. Tall green grasses and wildflowers.

Ahead of her a boy she guessed was seven or so was reaching for a poster on a telephone pole. His hands were sea anemones. He hopped and still couldn't quite get it. He needed rockets on his blue sneakers.

"Hi," Karin said, "Can I help you?"

Jumping wasn't getting him anywhere.

"Do you want me to get that for you?" The poster announced in bright pen and crayon:

CIRCUS, including today's date, and an address for a house a block away. When he drew it five days ago, he had high hopes of turning his house into somewhere with elephants and tigers and acrobats. He figured kids could leap out the kitchen window onto a stack of mattresses. There would be flags and balloons and strings of paper lanterns above carnival games in the backyard. Then he forgot about the circus. Until today.

The posters were promises he couldn't keep. He said he put one in the hall at school. And the school bus driver stopped on the morning route to tack one six feet up the telephone pole. But when the boy told his mom about them this morning, she said he better take them down. She said if anyone showed up, they might be disappointed by an ordinary house. A circus couldn't appear by magic, things didn't work that way. She told her son this would be a good day for them to take a drive and lay low.

"Well, you had a good idea," Karin said, "I'd love to see it happen someday."

He took the poster from her and thanked her. He had a few more to get. Then he could go home with them crumpled to his coat and wouldn't he be surprised to hear the calliope calling him to a house that had been turned into his dream-come-true. Like a Mother Goose picture book, there were boys and girls and animals running in and out.

12.

First, she heard birds. Twenty or thirty of them, trilling loud as telephones. Their aviary was clutched to a house on 19th like a butterfly net. One dawn when no one was looking, the house picked itself up and ran through Seattle and captured a flock of African finches and during the long gray wet raincoat of winter, they were kept inside the living room, warmed by radiators. They bided their time. They watched old movies on TV at night. They ordered seeds from catalogs. They played boardgames. They wrote letters to the *Times*. What about? Put twenty finches on a typewriter and find out.

It's a sign of spring as surely anticipated as blossoming when those birds finally tap from the house down a little ramp into their warm-weather quarters. When they are singing in the aviary, it becomes a screened Ray Bradbury porch that's trying without rocking-chairs and dandelion wine to lure summer near. Summer has a radio and lives below the equator and has to be coaxed north by songs and a change of heart. It needs to know it's wanted, why else would it travel all that way?

Those tropical birds are a postcard. Even trapped in a 10x10-foot plastic-covered mesh cage, they love to tell everyone that things are getting better. That's their message. Tomorrow might be cold and rainy again, there was still a lot of that weather waiting offshore and stored up in the hills, March, April, even into May and June, but it was alright once you got used to it and you realized it's just the season and it won't last forever. The ice is slowly melting.

Karin stopped on the sidewalk and held her bread in front of her poncho so it could see the muddy shapes of the birds dancing behind the opaque tarp and wire. It was sunny and they were singing like it was the start of spring. Someone could make a recording of it for the jukebox in the Western coffeehouse.

They weren't alone. Watching the birds from a flat stone in the garden, is a cat that was Lake City's great-great-great grandmother, a shadow of a shadow of a shadow of a cat-to-be.

13.

What do we remember about 1969 anyway? When I was little and we drove past the piers, I heard about the hotel where The Belateds stayed, and I could picture them fishing from the window. That's a memory that echoes to today. Even now, I can imagine the silver filament drifting in the air. Is everything that once happened just a ghost story? 1969 was a long time ago. 1964, a little more, 1965 too, and even 1992. Still, they were real and never really went away. Our world is planted with their buried treasure.

Some fantastic machine will be needed to dig back into the past and find them. In the 21st Century, the contraption will hover to the spot on 19th Street where a house once stood. A robot will place orange cones in a circle around it. A futuristic excavation takes place, prying layers of history, further, into the silt of a riverbed time keeps adding to. The machine will whir like a spinning quarter on a tabletop. A few people with nothing else to do will gather and watch it clawing past other memories. There goes last week, there goes 2002. Shoveling for a spark of gold.

This book will be found the same way, the fact that you are holding it, wherever you are, is proof of that. Maybe you found a copy left on a bus seat. Books show up in all sorts of places, a lost and found box, the libraries and bookstores, they can come as birthday presents. Sometimes you need to hunt for one that's rare as a rhinoceros.

Not all the treasure from the past ends up in museums. There are prospectors looking for those moments too. They sieve them out and put them in buckets and auction them off. For twelve million dollars, a mansion in Bel Air has a swimming pool holding a plesiosaur. Be careful though—that's not a scene you want to fall into. Fish swim around it and lizards fly overhead. It turns in the water eighty million years ago. Just wait until you see what the future has in store.

Until then, people will remember what happened on 19th Street like a dream until even those who were there will fade into a dream and what will be is only what's happening in the present, birds and running water and the wind pushing clouds.

14.

Each step took her closer to home and closer to another music, not bird or cat purring. A little further and she heard a song. Karin couldn't believe it. It followed her from the wax museum. It had a life of its own. It played every day on the radio, from cars passing by, a song you heard at the coffee shop or strummed on the corner guitar. She knew who it was—when the snow was falling, when it was raining, sunny or moonlit, their songs played in bedrooms when the door was closed and hearts were hypnotized. She hurried. The street was tipping her towards the music.

Cars were stopped in the road, doors were left open. Electricity wasn't contained in wires anymore, people were laughing and running down 19th in a current. It was happening, it was one of those miracles like the moon landing or the spring flowers rising from a cold ground. In the houses on either side of the street, windows were up, people with a view were leaning from their rooms and waving at the crowd. The sound echoed off the walls.

Karin slowed. She wanted to capture the moment, but it was like holding on to water as it flowed around her. Everything floated in the flood like the rain and melted snow that came down from the mountains and ended bunched together, pooled in front of her grandmother's boarding house. Why there? What was going on?

There are tidepools like this along the coastline. The ocean makes a low roar where little ponds in the rocks are formed, filled with other worlds, crabs, mussels, eel grass, barnacles. Small fish and starfish. Like a lighthouse keeper with a candle, she carried the bread that led her on a pilgrimage through the long day to this very moment, in the sunlight in the rush of a tide.

She laughed. It had to be real because there they were, the four of them, playing their song like a jukebox above the trees, and Hilda was standing next to them, holding a ukelele, up on the housetop in the sky with The Belateds.

3/15/24

The BELATEDS

Writing: January--March 2024

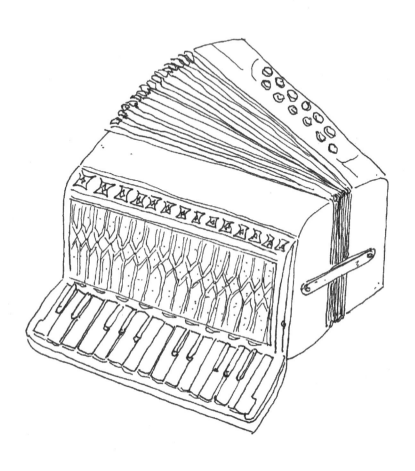

from *The Air Over Paris* (2023)

Books by Good Deed Rain

Saint Lemonade, Allen Frost, 2014. Two novels illustrated by the author in the manner of the old Big Little Books.

Playground, Allen Frost, 2014. Poems collected from seven years of chapbooks.

Roosevelt, Allen Frost, 2015. A Pacific Northwest novel set in July, 1942, when a boy and a girl search for a missing elephant. Illustrated throughout by Fred Sodt.

5 Novels, Allen Frost, 2015. Novels written over five years, featuring circus giants, clockwork animals, detectives and time travelers.

The Sylvan Moore Show, Allen Frost, 2015. A short story omnibus of 193 stories written over 30 years.

Town in a Cloud, Allen Frost, 2015. A three part book of poetry, written during the Bellingham rainy seasons of fall, winter, and spring.

A Flutter of Birds Passing Through Heaven: A Tribute to Robert Sund, 2016. Edited by Allen Frost and Paul Piper. The story of a legendary Ish River poet & artist.

At the Edge of America, Allen Frost, 2016. Two novels in one book blend time travel in a mythical poetic America.

Lake Erie Submarine, Allen Frost, 2016. A two week vacation in Ohio inspired these poems, illustrated by the author.

and Light, Paul Piper, 2016. Poetry written over three years. Illustrated with watercolors by Penny Piper.

The Book of Ticks, Allen Frost, 2017. A giant collection of 8 mysterious adventures featuring Phil Ticks. Illustrated throughout by Aaron Gunderson.

I Can Only Imagine, Allen Frost, 2017. Five adventures of love and heartbreak dreamed in an imaginary world. Cover & color illustrations by Annabelle Barrett.

The Orphanage of Abandoned Teenagers, Allen Frost, 2017. A fictional guide for teens and their parents. Illustrated by the author.

In the Valley of Mystic Light: An Oral History of the Skagit Valley Arts Scene, 2017. A comprehensive illustrated tribute. Edited by Claire Swedberg & Rita Hupy.

Different Planet, Allen Frost, 2017. Four science fiction adventures: reincarnation, robots, talking animals, outer space and clones. Cover & illustrations by Laura Vasyutynska.

Go with the Flow: A Tribute to Clyde Sanborn, 2018. Edited by Allen Frost. The life and art of a timeless river poet. In beautiful living color!

Homeless Sutra, Allen Frost, 2018. Four stories: Sylvan Moore, a flying monk, a water salesman, and a guardian rabbit.

The Lake Walker, Allen Frost 2018. A little novel set in black and white like one of those old European movies about death and life.

A Hundred Dreams Ago, Allen Frost, 2018. A winter book of poetry and prose. Illustrated by Aaron Gunderson.

Almost Animals, Allen Frost, 2018. A collection of linked stories, thinking about what makes us animals.

The Robotic Age, Allen Frost, 2018. A vaudeville magician and his faithful robot track down ghosts. Illustrated throughout by Aaron Gunderson.

Kennedy, Allen Frost, 2018. This sequel to *Roosevelt* is a coming-of-age fable set during two weeks in 1962 in a mythical Kennedyland. Illustrated throughout by Fred Sodt.

Fable, Allen Frost, 2018. There's something going on in this country and I can best relate it in fable: the parable of the rabbits, a bedtime story, and the diary of our trip to Ohio.

Elbows & Knees: Essays & Plays, Allen Frost, 2018. A thrilling collection of writing about some of my favorite subjects, from B-movies to Brautigan.

The Last Paper Stars, Allen Frost 2019. A trip back in time to the 20 year old mind of Frankenstein, and two other worlds of the future.

Walt Amherst is Awake, Allen Frost, 2019. The dreamlife of an office worker. Illustrated throughout by Aaron Gunderson.

When You Smile You Let in Light, Allen Frost, 2019. An atomic love story written by a 23 year old.

Pinocchio in America, Allen Frost, 2019. After 82 years buried underground, Pinocchio returns to life behind a car repair shop in America.

Taking Her Sides on Immortality, Robert Huff, 2019. The long awaited poetry collection from a local, nationally renowned master of words.

Florida, Allen Frost, 2019. Three days in Florida turned into a book of sunshine inspired stories.

Blue Anthem Wailing, Allen Frost, 2019. My first novel written in college is an apocalyptic, Old Testament race through American shadows while Amelia Earhart flies overhead.

The Welfare Office, Allen Frost, 2019. The animals go in and out of the office, leaving these stories as footprints.

Island Air, Allen Frost, 2019. A detective novel featuring haiku, a lost library book and streetsongs.

Imaginary Someone, Allen Frost, 2020. A fictional memoir featuring 45 years of inspirations and obstacles in the life of a writer.

Violet of the Silent Movies, Allen Frost, 2020. A collection of starry-eyed short story poems, illustrated by the author.

The Tin Can Telephone, Allen Frost, 2020. A childhood memory novel set in 1975 Seattle, illustrated by author like a coloring book.

Heaven Crayon, Allen Frost, 2020. How the author's first book *Ohio Trio* would look if printed as a Big Little Book. Illustrated by the author.

Old Salt, Allen Frost, 2020. Authors of a fake novel get chased by tigers. Illustrations by the author.

A Field of Cabbages, Allen Frost, 2020. The sequel to *The Robotic Age* finds our heroes in a race against time to save Sunny Jim's ghost. Illustrated by Aaron Gunderson.

River Road, Allen Frost, 2020. A paperboy delivers the news to a ghost town. Illustrated by the author.

The Puttering Marvel, Allen Frost, 2021. Eleven short stories with illustrations by the author.

Something Bright, Allen Frost, 2021. 106 short story poems walking with you from winter into spring. Illustrated by the author.

The Trillium Witch, Allen Frost, 2021. A detective novel about witches in the Pacific Northwest rain. Illustrated by the author.

Cosmonaut, Allen Frost, 2021. Yuri Gagarin stars in this novel that follows his rocket landing in an American town. Midnight jazz, folk music, mystery and sorcery. Illustrated by the author.

Thriftstore Madonna, Allen Frost, 2021. 124 summer story poems. Illustrated by the author.

Half a Giraffe, Allen Frost, 2021. A magical novel about a counterfeiter and his unusual, beloved pet. Illustrated by the author.

Lexington Brown & The Pond Projector, Allen Frost, 2022. An underwater invention takes three friends through time. Illustrated by Aaron Gunderson.

The Robert Huck Museum, Allen Frost, 2022. The artist's life story told in photographs, woodcuts, paintings, prints and drawings.

Mrs. Magnusson & Friends, Allen Frost, 2022. A collection of 13 stories featuring mystery and magic and ginkgo leaves.

Magic Island, Allen Frost, 2022. There's a memory machine in this magic novel that takes us to college.

A Red Leaf Boat, Allen Frost, 2022. Inspired by Japan, this book of 142 poems is the result of walking in autumn.

Forest & Field, Allen Frost, 2022. 117 forest and field recordings made during the summer months, ending with a lullaby.

The Wires and Circuits of Earth, Allen Frost, 2022. 11 stories from a train station pulp magazine.

The Air Over Paris, Allen Frost, 2023. This novel reveals the truth about semi-sentient speedbumps from Mars.

Neptunalia, Allen Frost, 2023. A movie-novel for Neptune, featuring mystery in a Counterfeit Reality machine. Illustrated by Aaron Gunderson.

The Worrys, Allen Frost, 2023. A family of weasels look for a better life and get it. Illustrated by Tai Vugia.

American Mantra, Allen Frost, 2023. The future needs poetry to sleep at night. Only one man and one woman can save the world. Illustrated by Robert Huck.

One Drop in the Milky Way, Allen Frost, 2023. A novel about retiring, with a little help from a skeleton and Abraham Lincoln.

Follow Your Friend, Allen Frost, 2023. A collection of animals from sewn, stapled, and printed books spanning 34 years of writing.

Holograms from Mars, Allen Frost, 2024. Married Martians try to make do on Earth in this illustrated novel.

The Belateds, Allen Frost, 2024. The Belateds came to Seattle in 1964 and left the four chapters in this novel.

Books by Bottom Dog Press

Ohio Trio, Allen Frost, 2001. Three short novels written in magic fields and small towns of Ohio. Reprinted as *Heaven Crayon* in 2020.

Bowl of Water, Allen Frost, 2004. Poetry. From the glass factory to when you wake up.

Another Life, Allen Frost, 2007. Poetry. From the last Ohio morning to the early bird.

Home Recordings, Allen Frost, 2009. Poetry. Dream machinery, filming Caruso, benign time travel.

The Mermaid Translation, Allen Frost, 2010. A bathysphere novel with Philip Marlowe.

Selected Correspondence of Kenneth Patchen, Edited by Larry Smith and Allen Frost, 2012. Amazing artist letters.

The Wonderful Stupid Man, Allen Frost, 2012. Short stories go from Aristotle's first car to the 500 dollar fool.

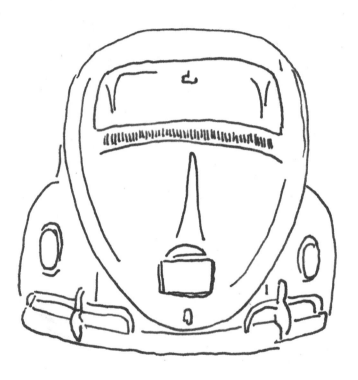